To Isabel, Jay, and the blue gentians of Linne Prairie

About This Book
The illustrations for this book were done in gouache watercolor on watercolor paper with digital enhancements.
This book was edited by Andrea Spooner, art directed by David Caplan, and designed by Prashansa Thapa.
The production was supervised by Kimberly Stella, and the production editor was Jen Graham.
The text was set in Brandon Grotesque, and the display type is hand-lettered.

Little
LAND

by
DIANA
SUDYKA

LB

LITTLE, BROWN AND COMPANY

NEW YORK • BOSTON

ONCE

there was a little bit of land.

It was not very big, like a mountain
that reaches up to the clouds.

It was not very tiny, like an island of moss
in the middle of a rushing creek.

It was somewhere in between
and just big enough for the life that lived upon it.

It had existed for a very long time.
It had not always looked as it does now.

Five hundred million years ago,
it may have looked like this.

Or sixty-seven million years ago,
a bit like this.

There was even a time, about one hundred thousand years ago,
when it was covered in thick layers of ice.
It was very cold, and life seemed to have left for good.

Eventually, over many years, the ice melted and water flowed, reshaping the land.

Life began anew.

Change was ever present, but one thing remained constant:
The land provided for all the life that lived upon it.

It provided soil rich
in nutrients to help
plants grow,

flowers with nectar for insects,

rivers for fish to swim in,

and food for birds,

bears, and
all other kinds
of animals

and their families.

Change was not always slow and small. Sometimes it was sudden and big.
A storm would come, a fire might start, and the land would burn.

Sometimes it burned so much that
what remained was no longer recognizable.

But even fire belonged to the land.

And eventually life and
land would find a way

to begin anew.

But some change does not belong to the land. It belongs to people.

Not so very long ago, people built a house on this little bit of land.

As the years passed, more people moved in.

More and more houses

and more and more buildings, factories, cars, and power plants were constructed.

Until the land was so covered, many rarely thought of it anymore . . .
except when they wanted to take from it.

Then they dug *into* the land, too,
for everything they needed
to make those buildings, factories,
cars, and power plants work.

At first no one noticed that there was a problem.

Well, maybe some did.

Change was slow in the beginning, but it gained power.

Life and land creaked and slid . . .

a tip, tip, tipping out of balance.

Every change was faster than the one
before, and it kept going until . . .

. . . it seemed unstoppable.

But even when things seem unstoppable,

unrecognizable,

and beyond repair . . .

. . . look closely,
and listen, too.

Can you hear the
little land talking
to you?

With help and care, life and land can find a way . . .

. . . to begin anew.

Do you know a little bit of land?

Is it in a backyard,
a forest, or a garden?

Maybe it is in a clay pot by your window.

It might be as small as an island of moss in a sidewalk crack.

Or is it much bigger and surrounded by stars?

No matter how big or little, you can take care of it.

And when you give love to something,

it will give back to you.

AUTHOR'S NOTE

Little Land was inspired by my love of nature and a deep desire to connect to place. I have spent years exploring everything from mountains down to the minutiae of my backyard. No matter where I am, the more I observe and listen, the more I feel connected to the ancient natural history of Earth. Humans are only a recent addition to that history, and yet we are living in a moment in which human activity is having a profound impact on climate and biodiversity. While our land will of course not literally turn upside down—as seen in the images in this book—forces on this planet are changing at a rate that are already overturning many norms of how people live.

I have been very moved by the writing of author and biologist Robin Wall Kimmerer, who talks about the idea of reciprocity with land—how Earth has always shared its gifts with us and how we need to give back to it in return. This story is about how believing in that concept leads to cultivating connection, and it is the first essential step to effectively decrease humanity's overwhelming impacts on the planet.

I live near Lake Michigan in North America. Maybe you live near me, or across an ocean. This book isn't specific to a particular place. I included plants and animals that can be found around where I live but also in other parts of the world. I hope that wherever you live, you can connect to a little bit of land and find ways to love and care for it.

SOME WORDS, CONCEPTS, AND QUESTIONS THAT INSPIRED THIS BOOK

biodiversity: The vast variety of species on Earth, which includes plants, animals, fungi, and bacteria. Earth is currently experiencing a dramatic loss of biodiversity caused by human activity. We need biodiversity to ensure stable, healthy systems of food, water, and shelter for all animals to survive, including humans.

biophilia: To be drawn to and to feel an affinity with nature. How can we nurture and preserve our innate connection to nature?

ecology: The study of the relationships between living organisms, including humans and their physical environment. What kinds of relationships do we have with different kinds of organisms?

ecosystem: The plants, animals, and other organisms in a geographical area and their interactions with the landscape and climate, which form a connected and complex web of life. What ecosystems do we live in or near?

reciprocity: A mutual, two-way exchange. How can we engage in reciprocity with the land?

stewardship: The responsible management of something entrusted to one's care. How can we be good stewards of Earth?

SOME ANIMALS AND PLANTS IN THIS BOOK (IN ORDER OF APPEARANCE)

horned lark: A species of ground-nesting bird that is found in North America, northern Europe, and Asia. Horned larks appear throughout the book, representing a living bridge between Earth's past and present. They span two different epochs and are still among us. In 2018, a preserved forty-six-thousand-year-old horned lark was found in the Siberian permafrost (http://www.sci-news.com/paleontology/horned-lark-siberian-permafrost-08151.html).

ammonite: An extinct group of marine mollusks that are closely related to octopuses and squid. They died out about sixty-six million years ago, and their fossils can be found in many parts of the world.

gentian: A type of flowering plant with roughly four hundred species found on all continents except Antarctica. The blue flowers in this book are based on an uncommon gentian species, the greater fringed gentian, native to North America. Many species of gentian are pollinated by bumblebee species, and their survival is dependent on intact ecosystems and pollinator populations.

humans (*Homo sapiens*): Humans are a very adaptable species of mammal, and as a result we are widespread and live in a range of habitats and climates. The understanding of our evolution is complex and changing, but current scientific thinking supports that modern *Homo sapiens* originated in Africa roughly three hundred thousand years ago. The early humans depicted in this book are Paleolithic hunter-gatherers who would have lived during the Last Glacial Period in parts of Europe and Asia. Groups of these people would have crossed over from Siberia into North America via the Beringia land bridge over twenty thousand years ago.

bumblebees and butterflies: Pollinating insects. There aren't a lot of bees and butterflies in the fossil record, but they may have evolved during the prehistoric Cretaceous period, when flowering plants evolved. Many pollinator insect species are currently in decline. Check out the Xerces Society for Invertebrate Conservation for information on how to help (https://xerces.org).

dinosaurs: Land-dwelling animals that evolved from egg-laying reptiles roughly 250 million years ago, dying off in large numbers around 65 million years ago. For dinosaur species that did survive, birds are their direct descendants.

crane: A species of long-legged and long-necked birds found in Africa, Asia, Australia, Europe, and North America. Modern crane species can be traced back roughly twenty million years in fossil records. As with the larks in this book, they represent a living bridge between Earth's past and present. Information on crane species and their conservation can be found at the International Crane Foundation (https://savingcranes.org).

woolly mammoth: A species of mammoth adapted to the cold environments of the Last Glacial Period that went extinct roughly four thousand years ago. Woolly mammoths lived across swaths of North America and northern Eurasia, coexisting with early humans.

bison: The largest surviving terrestrial mammals in both North America and Europe. Out of eight species, only the American bison and European bison (or wisent) remain. Both were hunted to near extinction. In 1952, wisent were reintroduced to a forest on the Polish-Belarus border. Through ongoing breeding and conservation efforts, the American bison's population has increased from abysmally low numbers due to nineteenth-century hunting.

oak: A tree family with many species having lobed or serrated leaves and producing acorns. There are roughly five hundred species worldwide. Fossil records of oaks date back fifty-five million years. Oaks are known as a keystone species, organisms that help maintain balance in an ecosystem. Roughly one-third of world oak species are under threat of extinction due to human activity. The Global Conservation Consortium is working to conserve all oak species (https://www.globalconservationconsortia.org/gcc/oak).

DIFFERENT EPOCHS REPRESENTED IN THIS BOOK (IN CHRONOLOGICAL ORDER)

epoch: An extended period of geologic time characterized by a distinctive development, such as a dominant life-form (dinosaurs, or humans) or geologic feature (glaciers).

Devonian period: Also known as the Age of Fishes, it spans roughly 419 million to 359 million years ago. Ammonites could be found swimming around during this time.

Cretaceous period: About 146 million to 66 million years ago. Dinosaurs dominated the land, but new groups of mammals, birds, and flowering plants also appeared.

Last Glacial Period: Marked by the advance and retreat of glaciers roughly 115,000 through 11,700 years ago. Large swaths of land, primarily in the Northern Hemisphere, were covered by massive ice sheets. Most of what remains of this ice is in Greenland and Antarctica.

Paleolithic: An extensive era in human history spanning roughly three million to eleven thousand years ago. It is marked by the development of stone tools and is usually split into three different periods: Lower, Middle, and Upper Paleolithic.

Holocene: Our current epoch, beginning about 11,700 years ago, after the end of the Last Glacial Period. It is characterized by the rapid growth and impact of humans worldwide, including the development of major civilizations and an overall transition toward living in urban areas.

Anthropocene: An unofficial period designation within the Holocene that is being used to describe this most recent period in Earth's history, when human activity is having a significant impact on Earth's climate, ecosystems, and overall biodiversity.

MORE RESOURCES

E. O. Wilson Biodiversity Foundation: E. O. Wilson was a scientist and environmentalist who spoke of humanity's urgent need to protect biodiversity. https://eowilsonfoundation.org.

iNaturalist: This website/app is an excellent resource for identifying organisms while outdoors exploring. https://www.inaturalist.org.

The National Geographic Society geologic time scale is an infographic depicting Earth's epochs in geologic time. https://www.nationalgeographic.org/media/age-earth/?utm_source=BibblioRCM_Row.

"Returning the Gift" by Robin Wall Kimmerer is an essay in which the author explains why gratitude is a powerful tool and outlines how we can reciprocate the gifts of Earth. https://www.humansandnature.org/earth-ethic-robin-kimmerer.